MR. TALL

by Roger Hargreaves

EGMONT

Mr Tall was very very very tall.

Quite the tallest person you've ever met.

In fact, quite the tallest person you've never met, because you've never met anybody with legs as long as Mr Tall's legs.

Have you?

Now, the problem with being as tall as Mr Tall was that life was just one long problem.

As you can see!

"Oh dear," he used to sigh.

"Oh dear me! I do so wish that my legs weren't quite so very very very long."

He decided to go for a walk to think over his problem.

He was just stepping over a tree when he heard a voice.

A little voice.

"Hello!"

It was Mr Small, standing underneath a daisy.

But Mr Tall was so tall he couldn't see him.

So Mr Small shouted at the top of his voice.

"Hello!"

A Mr Small shout is about as loud as a bee's sneeze.

So, it took quite some time for Mr Tall to spot him.

"Oh," he said gloomily, "it's you."

"You don't look very happy," said Mr Small.
"What's up?"

"I'm not," replied Mr Tall. "Because of these silly long legs of mine."

"Oh," said Mr Small.

Mr Small decided to cheer him up.

"Let's go for a walk together," he suggested.

So they did, which of course didn't work.

It was like a giraffe going for a walk with a mouse!

Then Mr Small had an idea.

Which did work!

And, because of the length of Mr Tall's legs, they very quickly walked all the way to the seaside.

"Come for a swim," cried Mr Small.

"Can't," replied Mr Tall. "By the time it gets deep enough for me to swim I'll be out the other side."

So Mr Small went for a swim, while Mr Tall sat down with a face which was nearly as long as his legs.

Mr Tickle came along.

"Hello," he said. "You look as if you need cheering up. Care for a tickle?"

"No thanks," replied Mr Tall. "What I would care for are some different legs. Mine are much too long."

"So are my arms," said Mr Tickle cheerfully. "But all the better for tickling!"

And off he went, chuckling, looking for somebody to tickle.

Looking for anybody to tickle!

Mr Nosey came along.

"Cheer up," he said. "You look very down in the mouth. What's the problem?"

"It's my legs," replied Mr Tall. "They're too long!"

"So's my nose," replied Mr Nosey, laughing. "But all the better for poking into other people's business!"

And he went off, looking for something to be nosey about.

Looking for anything to be nosey about.

Mr Greedy came along.

"Hello," he cried. "You look gloomy! What's wrong?"

"It's my legs," explained Mr Tall. "They're too big!"

"So is my tummy," replied Mr Greedy. "But all the better for filling with food!"

And off he went, licking his lips.

Mr Tall sat there and thought about Mr Tickle's arms, and Mr Nosey's nose, and Mr Greedy's tummy.

He smiled.

And then, he grinned.

And then, he laughed out loud.

He looked at his legs, those very very very long legs of his.

"All the better for walking," he chuckled.

And walked home.

In four minutes.

Forty miles!

Mr Small came out of the sea after his short swim.

"And how am I going to get home?" he asked himself.

So he set off walking.

All the way home.

Forty miles!

That was last year.

He got home yesterday!